KINDNESS IS ALL AROUND

Olga Venosa & Giuliana Savino

Dedicated to my adorable niece and nephew,

Anna and Daniele,

whom I love more than anything else in this world.

TABLE OF CONTENTS

ABOUT THE AUTHORS AND THE BOOK

Dear Reader, I am so thrilled we are about to begin this journey together.

Let's start by introducing myself. My name is Olga Venosa, no, I am not Russian, and I know Olga sounds quite a Nordic name, right? But I am actually Italian, born in a beautiful seaside city called Bari, in the south of Italy, in 1980. A few years ago I also became a British citizen, after spending over 14 years working in the wonderful multi-cultural city that is London. My love of languages (I now speak 6) has given me the chance to learn about other cultures. It has become one of the most exciting things in life, and I have found so many opportunities in London!

I had a very difficult childhood, but one thought that always kept me going was, "there's always a sunny day after a storm, so it must be true for my life too." I truly believe anything is possible, and despite a lot of sad moments and hard times in my life, I felt very lucky because I was able to get through anything with a smile. I have learned that even when we feel alone, we have beautiful, caring, and loving people around us. We just need to be patient and open.

Along my journey, I bumped into someone who became my great friend, Giuliana Savino. Giuliana is a psychologist and psychotherapist who specialises in multiculturalism, which is the way people who come from different parts of the world behave towards each other.

Giuliana has worked with Italian TV channels like RAI and MEDIASET, (they are like the BBC in the UK or CNN in the US). If you wonder if Giuliana knows lots of celebrities... the answer is yes, she does!! You should have seen my face when she told me that. I thought, "... oohhh WOW!!"

One day Giuliana and I were talking and decided we wanted to write a book for children, and here we are together fulfilling that dream.

I have written the first story, which is based on my true life, while the other two stories have been co-written by myself and Giuliana.

While writing the book, luck knocked at my door again, and I bumped into Domenico Meleleo, pediatrician and nutritionist. That means he is an expert in food and children. Yes, he could play with you and make sure everyone has lots of fun, but he can also make you feel strong and make your energy last longer by telling you what to eat! So Interesting!

So, I showed him this book and asked him to provide nutritional guidance and advice to help you children always feel great!

Domenico has developed a lot of projects and has done some very important work for the Italian Government Department of Health & Social Care and some Italian scientific societies.

So, I would like to thank Domenico, our Illustrator Glen Holman, known for his Netflix and other international works, and also the amazing, We Are Stronger Charity's volunteers Lisa Crivello and Lucy Gibson, who helped me with the proofreading of the English version of this book, and all the incredible work they are doing with my charity.

I decided to found We Are Stronger in 2017, it is an anti-bullying and anti-violence charity that helps anyone in need. I chose the name because I believe we are stronger than the feeling of bullying others and those who bully.

This was my childhood dream. You see, more than one dream can become true!

Always believe and never give up!

Olga Venosa

Giuliana Savino

SMILING PENNY AND HER WORLD OF KINDNESS

In a small town by the sea, there lived a little girl named Penny. She had black curly hair, big brown eyes, and a beautiful smile. She loved living by the seaside, and would spend each day playing with her friends on the beach.

One sunny day, Penny was out with her brother and friends on their favourite beach, playing in the sand, where you could hear the splashing of the sea. She was a lively and loving child and easily won people over with her adoring nature, kindness, and innocence.

Penny used to daydream about what life would be like when she grew up. She wanted to work in a big skyscraper with views as far as the eye could see.

She used to sleep with her pocket money, thinking she would make it grow by collecting and saving small coins.

Penny was top of the class at school! Maths was her favourite subject, and she was unbeatable in her ability to make quick calculations in her head.

The little girl and her dad would often play a game together when walking down the street. Her dad would pick a word on a sign and ask Penny to pronounce it backwards whilst he counted down the seconds. She had to say the word in this funny way before time ran out. She got especially good at this, getting quicker and quicker every time before her dad could finish counting.

Penny also loved dancing. She would imagine being a ballerina on a big stage with beaming lights, performing in front of a large audience. She would dance for hours and never stop, feeling the music burning from her feet. Goosebumps would run all across her body until this incredible feeling of happiness would fill her completely.

One night, when no one was around, a shadow from far away crept up closer to where little Penny was sleeping. She was resting beautifully and peacefully in her bed when the shadow woke her up. She was scared, but the shadow opened a bag full of candies and chocolates and told her,

"Do not worry, everything is ok. Here, take some goodies."

She replied, "I don't want to. I would like to sleep."

The shadow whispered, "Hush! Do not raise your voice and do not worry, there is no need for you to be scared. This will be our secret. I am here because you are special. Now why don't you try the candy, my dear." Insisting, he made her eat and eat until Penny felt bad and her belly was hurting.

The next day, she was feeling unwell, but she was ashamed to tell anyone that she had been eating sweets all night, especially because the shadow told her not to mention their secret to anyone.

When night fell again, the shadow sneaked into Penny's room without getting

noticed by her parents and asked her to keep quiet while reopening the bag full of goodies. This time it made her eat even more, and even though she was full up, it forced her to keep eating until she felt sick again.

Days passed, and every night the shadow returned. Soon, Penny started to feel like she wanted that bag full of goodies earlier, and so the shadow would appear during the day as well. While all other children were outside running and playing, Penny was spending more and more time with the shadow eating candies until feeling sick. One day she started to feel guilty. She was scared, ashamed, felt ugly and fat. She couldn't recognise herself. She didn't like herself anymore.

Penny started to find it difficult to wake up in the morning, and she would find excuses not to go to school. She would look in awe at the other children and think to herself, "They all look so carefree and happy, so beautiful. Why am I not like them? Are they born that way?" Penny felt different and wondered why.

She would feel lonely with no friends. She started thinking perhaps no one liked her anymore. She began to think that the others had realised she was spending all her time eating sweets, and now they were ignoring her. Penny would think, "Why has the shadow chosen me? I don't want to be special! Why me?"

Penny spent hours crying in a small corner of a room, where no one would notice her. She couldn't do her homework any longer and was finding it difficult to concentrate. "How can it be possible that everything used to be so easy for me, but now it all seems so difficult? Why? I don't understand."

Penny thought she could feel everyone looking at her. She wasn't comfortable with her body and the way she looked and felt anymore. She slowly began to spend more time on her own. Her friends began to spread rumours about her. She was no longer invited to birthday parties or playground games. All that Penny had left was her dancing, which still bought her moments of pure joy.

One day, Penny was in ballet class. Her teacher was talking about the story of Romeo and Juliet and their secret love. He mentioned how the secret made their love complicated and ended in tragedy, so Penny asked, "Mr Dominique, I thought it was good to keep a secret if someone asks us to, right?"

The teacher answered, "Well, no, not if it is about something that causes pain or suffering. If it doesn't feel right, then we shouldn't keep it secret. We should always tell someone older we love, like your parents, or myself, or anyone you trust, who loves you, and ask for advice."

On her way home, she was walking across the beach when Penny noticed something glowing in the dark a

few meters ahead. As she edged closer, the little girl curiously reached for that ray of light and discovered a beautiful heart-shaped crystal-covered book. She sat down on the sand and opened it up. The first page said, "Trust and entrust, love and kindness are found when you believe. There are great people in this world. We can meet them too. Luck brings you here." Penny looked towards the sea, where all the big bright stars were reflected in the water. Mr Dominique's words went round and round in her mind, carrying her away on the sound of the waves. She suddenly knew everything would be OK.

The next day, Penny hurried to her ballet class and arrived earlier than usual. As she reached the studio, she could hear Mr Dominique listening to his collection of new musical pieces.

She gently tapped on the open door, leaned inside, and whispered,

"Hi, Mr Dominique, can I come in? I have something I would like to tell you."

Mr Dominique replied, "Of course, my little swan, come in!"

Penny timidly walked into the studio. As she edged closer, she began to feel more and more nervous. She was shaking! It was at that moment when she burst into tears. Mr Dominique was taken aback and looked surprised. He took her hand and gently said,

"What happened, my little girl? Why are you crying?"

Penny answered, "Because I have to tell you a secret. I did something I hated, and I didn't want to do it, but I was forced to."

"Tell me, Little Penny, you can confide in me, tell me what happened." Mr Dominique said calmly.

He was such a kind gentleman, and Penny felt she could trust him.

"You know the shadow... that shadow..." Penny sobbed.

"Carry on, my little girl."

Penny found her strength and continued, "The shadow makes me eat lots of sweets when no one else is there. I told him that I don't want to, but he doesn't leave me alone. He visits every night and stuffs me so much that my belly aches. He told me he had chosen me because I am special, and I had to keep it secret. But I don't want to be special, Mr Dominique! Now I feel ugly, fat, and awful. Please help me. I don't know what to do."

Tears were streaming down Penny's face. Although she was upset, she felt so relieved after telling someone about her secret. Mr Dominique stretched out his arms and embraced her with the biggest hug. He then took Penny's hand, looked into her eyes, and gently said, "You do not need to worry anymore, my dear. The shadow will not appear again. If anyone similar comes along, just say I will call Mr Dominique. He protects me and knows all my secrets. I promise you, Penny, no one will ever make you feel this way again. You are very special, and this is a good thing, but being special should not make you feel bad. You are beautiful, and everyone loves you. You have nothing to be ashamed about. You love studying. You love dancing and playing on the beach with your brother and friends. Everything will get back to normal, and you will be happy and full of energy. All will soon look brighter and beautiful again. I love you, my little Penny. You are safe now."

As soon as Penny's mother arrived to pick her up, the little girl ran towards her. Her eyes were full of tears, and she squeezed her mum tight.

"I love you, mummy, please hug me."

Penny's mother was puzzled about why Penny was crying but hugged her back and asked, "What happened, my baby? Are you OK?"

"I love you," Penny repeated whilst holding on to her mother.

Her mother kissed her daughter tenderly and replied

"I love you too, my baby. I love you so much."

Mr Dominique told Penny's mother what had happened. She was shocked, but relieved that her daughter had the courage to speak up and tell him the secret. In that moment she realised what Penny had been through and why Penny's behaviour had recently changed. Now everything became clear.

Her mother talked to the other parents, and together they all decided to have a party for the children. They also agreed that from then on, every child would be invited and welcomed, with no exceptions.

The day of the party arrived. The room was decorated with colourful balloons, beautiful flowers, many toys and games. In the back garden, there was a big round trampoline and a pool. Music was playing, and a wonderful smell filled the room. The sumptuously laid tables were covered with chocolate, blueberry cupcakes, apple pies, crisps, pizzas, candies, and ice cream. The children entered the hall with astonishment and excitement! One by one, they started to run towards the toys and games. Penny was close to the biggest box of toys and started smiling as she played with her friends. In just one moment, she had forgotten all the bad things that had happened before.

Suddenly, the children formed a circle holding hands. They reached out to Penny who smiled and joined them. They all began to sing and dance together. Penny never felt happier.

Before she knew it, the party was over. Penny was excited and filled with joy from the wonderful time with her friends. On her way home in the car with her mother, she was looking out the window, daydreaming and feeling so content. She turned and smiled at her mother, who asked her,

"Did you enjoy the party, my little girl? I saw that you played with all your friends. Did you talk to them too?"

Penny's eyes widened, and she replied,

"Yes mummy, they told me that they thought I didn't like them anymore, as I spent so much time by myself. But they were glad I was back with them as they have always been my friends, and they love me very much. I am so happy, mummy. It was a very beautiful day for me. Can we take all the remaining food to the homeless? They don't have anything, so let's go and help them".

Her mother looked at her and smiled, "Of course, dear, that is a lovely idea."

They took all the leftover party food to a well-known street where the homeless were sitting around on the pavement. Penny gave them a big smile as she handed out the food, saying,

"Today I have been very lucky, now it is your turn."

The homeless thanked her for her kindness and waved goodbye when she walked away with her mother.

When Penny and her mother arrived home, everything felt different. It was even better than before. Something magical had happened.

Penny was still smiling when she went to bed. The moonlight was bright, and a pleasant sense of calm filled her room. The little girl finally fell into a peaceful and restful sleep.

A SPRINKLE OF SWEETNESS

Lucas was a lively and happy child who adored cakes. He lived in Stanton, a quaint little village in the English County of Gloucestershire. He had a great passion for cooking. This passion had been passed to him by his mother. He would always follow her around in the kitchen, especially when she was making desserts. He had become so good at baking cakes that his mother often said kindly, "Lucas, you outshine me. Your hands are magical." She added, "Since you have become so good during the summer holidays, why don't we showcase your cakes at the famous Stanton market? This is where great pastry Chefs and Cooks come together from all over the world."

Lucas's specialty was the chocolate roll, which he named 'Smiling Choc' because it reminded him of a chocolate smile. Smiling Choc was one of his favourite treats. In fact, he not only loved cooking it but also eating it in large quantities along with all his other delights.

Every day, people would stop curiously when they passed in front of his stall. The chocolate roll had a tasty cream filling and was a popular choice with the children who really loved sugar.

There were two other stalls next to Lucas's, run by two other children called Mark and Violet. Mark's stall had plain croissants, which were eaten by children who liked savory pastries, whilst Violet's had homemade muffins, which were chosen by the children who had a bit more of a sweet tooth.

Mark had a crush on the beautiful Violet, and in his attempts to gain her attention and appear clever, he enjoyed making fun of Lucas by calling him "Fat". Once Mark got started poking fun at Lucas, he was able to laugh at him for hours. This made Lucas feel insecure and self-conscious. He hoped every day to become thinner and thought to himself, "If I manage to contain my appetite, Mark will stop laughing at me." One day, Violet was watching the two companions arguing as Mark was teasing Lucas. Lucas was upset and said to Mark, "Why do you always say mean things to me? It's horrible, and I do not like it."

Mark simply replied, "Oh, you know I'm only joking! Try not to be so sensitive. It's only a bit of fun."

Although Violet didn't like the way Mark treated Lucas and could see it really upset him, she said nothing. Unfortunately, Mark continued to tease Lucas every morning until he felt even worse.

The more time passed, the more unbearable the situation became. One day Lucas decided, that he had to do something. He wanted to find a solution and in order to stop Mark's insults, he came up with an idea. He would start adding a layer of soft and light icing sugar grains onto his sweet chocolate rolls. With a little help from the north wind, the sugar would blow around and would spread sweetness over everyone, including Mark.

Lucas thought that this was the only way to silence Mark by treating him with kindness. The very next morning, Lucas went on with the plan and noticed that the children really loved his new sugary cakes. That little extra sweetness made his treats all the more appealing.

Mark watched in amazement as Lucas became so successful. Now, whenever he tried to make fun of him, Lucas got the north wind to blow sugar all over him. Violet had also seen the success of Lucas's new cakes and began to take more notice of him. She now realised how clever he was.

Mark was hard hit by Lucas' success. He spent his days feeling jealous, not just of the way the children loved the sugary chocolate rolls but also of all the attention Violet was now giving Lucas. But what astonished Mark most was that since his plain croissants had been covered with Lucas's icing sugar, they too were becoming more popular with the children.

The thought occurred to Mark that he had never really known sweetness in his life. He realised it was Lucas, the one he had mocked and humiliated for so long, who had introduced him to it. Mark asked himself why he behaved that way to Lucas, when all he had done was treat him with kindness and compassion.

As the days passed, Mark began to feel admiration for Lucas and to look at him differently. But he still couldn't understand how the person he had repeatedly made fun of was giving him something so precious in return, sweetness.

One day Mark gathered up the courage to approach Lucas. He asked him,

"Why do you sprinkle my croissants with your sugar, especially after I've behaved towards you so badly? I knew that you didn't like being laughed at, and still I continued."

Lucas thought about this for a moment and replied, "That's right, you hurt me, but even when I was suffering, I always knew inside me that you were suffering too. One day I realized that to make you stop, I would have to give you a little of my sweetness.

I wanted you to know that sweetness is not only in the sugar, but it is in our actions and a part of our soul that has the power to bring joy to everyone around us. I knew if I gave you some sweetness, you would pass it on to even more people. I believe that everyone deserves a little sweetness in their life, and there is nothing better than spreading it yourself. Now that you have tried it and received it, I'm sure that you, too, will be encouraged to be good and treat others with kindness. I am sure you will see that everything will then become more beautiful."

Mark listened to Lucas carefully and began to understand the importance of kindness. He realised that when one person acts kindly to another, it encourages that person to also be kind. So, your one act of kindness then spreads out further and further.

Mark was touched by Lucas' words. He told him, "I would like to keep a little of your sweetness forever. I did notice the children around my stall used to look bored and sad, but now I see they smile at my croissants as they smile at your cakes."

Mark continued, "You have managed not only to surround me with sweetness but also to fill my empty heart with love. Thank you for showing me this simple gesture of goodwill. I appreciate and respect you so much for showing patience when you could have been unkind to me as I have been to you."

From that day on, Lucas continued to sprinkle some of his sugar on Mark's cakes. He had finally understood that he shouldn't be ashamed of his sweetness.

He knew his sweetness was a great gift that he should show with pride.

Mark felt much happier after talking with Lucas and said, "Thank you, Lucas. I don't think I can thank you enough." He thought for a moment and then added, "How silly I have been for laughing at you, but I realise now that my laughter came from my emptiness. I thought that by making fun of you, and making you suffer, I myself would become stronger. But instead, I became more fragile and sad. You taught me that only love can bring us closer to others and make us happy. Often, we are afraid of opening up to others because we are afraid that they will hurt us. We treat them badly because we think it will make us feel better.

When you covered my croissants with sugar, your gesture touched my heart, and I understood many things. For the first time, I understood the meaning of friendship. Your love has filled me and makes me want to spread joy to others."

Violet, who had always stayed out of discussions before, overheard what the boys were saying and decided to speak up. She told them, "I have also been wrong. I should have said or done something instead of watching and staying silent. Now I have realised that my silence was hurtful to you, Lucas, and I am sorry for that. I didn't have the courage to ask Mark to stop with his jokes and giggles. I was afraid that he might tease me too, so it was safer for me to be his friend. But I should have said what I thought and stood up for you. I could have stopped Mark from making fun of you and shown that I was courageous and wise and above all a good friend."

"I think we have all learned something from this experience," said Lucas. "We have seen the beauty of our friendship and that we can only find happiness by giving love to others."

From that day on, everything changed, the childrens' friendship made their market stalls even more popular. Lucas became happier. He felt loved and appreciated and decided to eat only one small dessert a day. He shared it with his friends and even gave away some of his cakes to the people in the village. In return, they brought him fruit, vegetables, meat, fish, and many other fresh foods. As he ate this food, he began to feel even stronger than before. The friendship and sweetness he had given to Mark had not only returned to him but had helped him be more confident in himself. Since then, the friends became inseparable.

WE ARE STRONGER TOGETHER

In a colourful field by a hill near a secluded forest, an old lady named Nora Heartbell was known for her kindness and incredible cooking skills. She lived in the family house built by her great great grandfather. Her garden was of astonishing beauty, full of flowers and butterflies. Nora had no knowledge that three tiny elves also lived there. Every evening as the sunset, they would find a way to creep into her home by putting together a miniature ladder. They would climb through the kitchen window and steal Nora's home-cooked delicacies.

Nora could not understand why her food was going missing. One evening she decided to hide in the cupboard with the door slightly ajar so that she could see what pesky thing kept eating her treats.

As the sun set, the elves came out feeling very hungry! They immediately got their ladder and clambered through the kitchen window as usual.

They jumped down, and Nora could not believe her eyes! There were three adorable little elves eating her food. Instead of anger or frustration, Nora's heart grew with love. They were clearly hungry and needed help, and she wanted to take care of them. So, every evening, Nora would wait in hiding until the elves came out to eat her food, and each day, she grew fonder of her new friends. She even started cooking extra food as she discovered that each elf had its own particular tastes and needs.

The three elves were called Gael, Arel, and Caden. They came from very different backgrounds with physical characteristics which set them apart from each other. Gael was tall and sporty and ate everything, but above all, he loved wheat pasta, meat, and cheese. Caden was athletic and very flexible. However, like the rest of his family, eating wheat made him feel ill, so he preferred to eat rice or potatoes with his meat and fish. Finally, there was Arel, who was strong but shorter and a little heavier than the other two elves. He had a huge appetite and loved to eat everything, particularly chicken and fish. He was told by the forest fairy that if he got very hungry, he should eat lots of brown rice, fruit, and vegetables instead of white bread and cakes, and Arel found that he felt more energetic and awake when he did this.

One evening, when the sun went down, the three elves were feeling particularly hungry. So, they began to climb their ladder. They quickly realized that something was wrong. With eating all the lovely food Nora had been making them, they had grown a great deal in the last few months. The ladder could not cope with all their extra weight and broke, causing them to come crashing down to the ground with a hard 'THUD.' The three elves sat in the garden for several hours, wondering what to do. They realised that Nora must have fallen asleep and had not noticed their absence. They became sad at the thought of this and set about making a plan for getting through the kitchen window without the ladder.

As Gael was the tallest and strongest of the three, he convinced himself that he could go up alone and eat all Nora's food by himself. He was so confident about being able to do this on his own that he began to make fun of Arel, saying,

"You are small and fat. You will never be able to climb up without a ladder, but I am strong and agile, and with my cunning plan, I shall reach the window in no time at all!"

Arel, who was quite shy, sat in silence. He felt sad and discouraged that Gael could be right.

Caden watched all this without saying a word. He felt upset by what Gael was saying but didn't know what to do.

Then Gael turned to Caden and said, "You are sporty like me, so you might be able to climb up to the kitchen but stay away from me. My family doesn't like yours. You are so different from us that we keep guys like you at a distance."

This time, Caden did not hold back and angrily replied, "I might be different to you, but the elves in my family are very special and proud. You know, before we stopped eating wheat, we often were in a sad mood. We were tired and irritable and almost always had stomach aches. We didn't have the energy to play with the other elves, but now, with gluten-free food, you can see how we run and jump happily with our friends. You cannot imagine how satisfying it is feeling good after having been sick for a long time."

Gael thought about this for a while and then replied, "No, you're the one who doesn't understand. My family is so successful we are known all over the world. I must be superior to you two. Look at me, how healthy and strong I grow. I am not like Arel or you. I wasn't fat, and I wasn't ill either."

Caden listened to him and then replied, "Your problem is you are too full of yourself. Since your family got famous, you have begun to look down on us, telling us that we know nothing and should keep quiet. But the reality is that the other elves don't like you anymore. They know you only think about yourself and you don't care about them. You're not so special, but lots of celebrities are gluten-free like me, including athletes who have won many competitions. So, you can also stop thinking so highly about yourself, and acting as if you know everything about everyone, and attacking us for everything."

Arel listened to the two elves arguing, but he didn't want to join in. He just wanted to go home to his family, where he felt loved and protected.

Gael ignored Caden and got up. He tried to stretch up to the window, but he wasn't tall enough, so he slipped and fell. It was still a big challenge for a little elf, but he was too proud to stop. However, after a couple of hours he realized that he couldn't do it on his own. It was then that he had an idea. He turned to Caden and said, "You're nearly as tall as me. If we climb one on top of the other, we should reach the edge of the window."

Caden was confused. Why was Gael asking for his help when he had just said those horrible things to him? He thought about it a while and then said to Gael, "You don't even deserve an answer from me, but at least, you now realise you are not so powerful on your own. I forgive you for all the poisonous things you said to me because you have asked me for help, and I am sure that you too, will understand that forgiving is the first step. But I think we also need Arel's help. He is strong and heavy and will give us a solid base and an upward push. Together, we can be stronger and reach the window. The problem is that I don't know how we could help Arel to get up at the end."

The two elves started to think for a way. Arel, who had been listening, told them, "Don't worry about me, I will help you both despite Gael's unkind words. I loved what you said, Caden. I too forgive Gael. You see, I was once saved by the forest fairy when I was in serious danger. The fairy explained to me that sometimes we can't see the wonder of the universe because we are too busy thinking about all our own worries and desires. I may be the silent type, but sometimes you need to be still and silent to see things through the heart."

Gael was a little confused but also annoyed. He asked, "What are you talking about? How can you see with your heart when it doesn't have eyes?"

Arel replied, "You must close your eyes and cover your ears with your hands. When the colours and noises of the world around you fade away, only then will your heart be able to see."

Gael turned to the wall, squeezed his eyes shut and covered his ears tightly with his hands. At first he couldn't see or hear anything but eventually, the image of Arel appeared in front of him. He looked different from normal, and he had a special light. Gael stared for a while longer and saw that the light came from Arel's kindness and his generosity in offering to help his two fellow elves without asking for anything in return.

"I am seeing through my heart!" He screamed with great surprise. "I can see you, Arel, you are a special and generous elf, and you are always there for others. I wish I was more like you."

Arel replied, "Well, I wish I had your determination! I could never have thought up that plan to reach the window without the ladder. You see, I have something that you do not have, and you have something that I do not have. We are both unique and special in our own ways."

Gael understood at that moment that even though they were different, they were all fantastic beings. The three hugged each other tightly as Gael began to cry.

"Why are you crying?" Arel asked him.

"Because I realise how silly I was to think that I was better than you, just because I was tall and sporty. I thought I was so clever that I could do everything on my own. Please forgive me, Arel."

Arel replied: "It is true, we all need each other, and together we can do great things. Perhaps if we ask my fairy friend for help too, we can all get back into the kitchen."

Caden, who had followed the conversation between the two with interest, said, "Arel, I think you are the wisest, and since you are the one who knows the fairy well, I think it is better if you talk to her."

So Arel called the fairy, by twisting his hat so the bell on the end, made a beautiful sound, and the fairy appeared immediately. "Hi Arel. How are you? And what can I do for you?"

He told her what happened, explaining: "Dear Forest fairy, my sweet friend, please help us. Our ladder is broken, and we can't get into Nora's kitchen anymore. We are so hungry! Gael had a plan to get in,

but it meant I would have been left behind. Now he had realised that we all need to be together, so I am asking you to help the three of us."

The kind-hearted fairy turned to him and said, "Dear Arel, you are a good and kind elf, and I will help by giving you all small wings. But you must hurry and learn to fly quickly, as the wings will not last long."

The fairy waved her magic wand, and the three elves found two small wings on their backs, but they soon acknowledged that it was very difficult to learn to fly in a short time. No matter how many times they tried flying up to the window, they kept finding themselves on the ground again.

Arel understood that they were all too weak from hunger to learn to fly, and he was especially afraid that Gael and Caden would get hurt. He turned again to the fairy and said, "Dear fairy of the forest, thank you for giving us wings, but as you can see, we can't fly well enough to reach the kitchen window. I think I have a better idea! I can now hear Nora is in the kitchen. Can you get her attention so she can see us?"

The fairy laughed and said, "Dear Arel, you are so cute, and I really enjoyed seeing you all try to fly. It reminded me of when my wings first grew. I was just the same! But you are very smart, and this idea seems easier. I will rattle the window shutters." After a while, the little elves saw Nora coming to the window to see what the noise was. She immediately saw her three elves were cold and hungry as they couldn't reach the window. So, this time she opened the door for them, smiling. She welcomed her friends inside and gave them their favorite dishes, which the elves devoured greedily. The fairy was happy to see the three elves safe and sound, enjoying their food, so she flew back to the forest to carry on her magic fairy work.

From that day on, the three elves would get together every day and tell each other many stories about their lives. Sometimes no one could hear them, because they had learned to speak through their hearts. A simple look between them was often enough to understand each other.

COOKING ACTIVITY

Through the kindness' door...

Violet: "I am so happy to be here with you, my friends, aren't you?"

Mark: "Yes, I am too. We all are!"

Violet: "Let's have more fun. We need to tell the reader to pick a recipe they love and cook it with their loved ones."

Mark: "Yes! Dear Reader, first of all, thank you for reading all of our stories, we hope that you enjoyed them. Now you have to choose your favourite recipe, and play the Chef game with whoever you want! It could be your friends, your family, and your teachers, anyone ready to take on this challenge with you. We promise it is going to be fun!"

Penny: "Friends, I want to play too, but before choosing our recipe, let's think a bit. I have noticed that if I eat too much, my body slows down, and I can't move properly, but if I don't eat, I don't have the energy for dancing. So, I need to eat the right amount before my ballet class." Gael: "Yes! My little Penny to have the right energy for dancing or any sport, my coach told me to eat just the right amount of food for breakfast or lunch, just a couple of hours before your training."

Lucas: "I have noticed that after my sports training, I can get my strength back quickly if I have any of the following: fruity milkshake, a piece of cake, milk, and biscuits, or a small sandwich isn't that great!"

Caden: "Oh yes, Lucas, and have you realised that if you're not training, it only takes one fruit or yogurt to

feel energised! I love that food can help us with our daily strength."

Gael: "Dear friends, let me tell you a secret. Whenever I win a sports medal, it's been after eating food like vegetables, legumes, fruits, cereals, or fish. I am sure it helps me win too."

Arel: "Yes, Gael, my football coach won lots of medals too, and he told me he was always eating the food you listed. This is a great tip! Thanks a lot! I will try myself too."

Penny: "Food is our greatest companion!"

All together: "So dear Reader, what are you waiting for? Go to the next page, pick your ingredients and start planning your cooking trip! Enjoy it and have a wonderful time! Remember, no matter what, always Smile!"

Recipe

Recipe Name

....

Ingredients

....
....
....

Directions

....
....
....
....
....
....
....
....
....
....
....
....

Printed in Great Britain
by Amazon